1866 - 1991

125th

ANNIVERSARY

TWIN
SURPRISES

Here's a list of some other
Redfeather Books from Henry Holt

———————

The Class with the Summer Birthdays
by Dian Curtis Regan

*Max Malone and the Great Cereal Rip-off
by Charlote Herman

Max Malone Makes a Million
by Charlotte Herman

*Snakes Are Nothing to Sneeze At
by Gabrielle Charbonnet

*Something Special
by Emily Rodda

Stargone John
by Ellen Kindt McKenzie

Teddy B. Zoot
by J. Clarke

213 Valentines
by Barbara Cohen

*Available in paperback

TWIN SURPRISES

Susan Beth Pfeffer

Illustrated by Abby Carter

A Redfeather Book

Henry Holt and Company · New York

Text copyright © 1991 by Susan Beth Pfeffer
Illustrations copyright © 1991 by Abby Carter
First edition
Published by Henry Holt and Company, Inc.,
115 West 18th Street, New York, New York 10011.
Published simultaneously in Canada by Fitzhenry & Whiteside Ltd.,
195 Allstate Parkway, Markham, Ontario L3R 4T8.

Library of Congress Cataloging-in-Publication Data
Pfeffer, Susan Beth.
    Twin surprises / Susan Beth Pfeffer ; illustrated by Abby Carter.
    (A Redfeather book)
    Summary: Relates Betsy's humorous efforts to keep a surprise
birthday party for her twin sister a secret.
    ISBN 0-8050-1850-6
                    Fiction.   2. Sisters—Fiction.   3. Birthdays—Fiction.
                              L. Carter, Abby, ill.
                    Redfeather
PZ   1991
[E]   dc20   91-13968

Henry Holt books are available at special discounts
for bulk purchases for sales promotions, premiums,
fund-raising, or educational use. Special editions
or book excerpts can also be created to specification.

Printed in the United States of America
on acid-free paper.∞

10   9   8   7   6   5   4   3   2   1

To my mother, Freda,
in honor of her 80th birthday
—S. B. P.

Contents

1

A Surprise for Crista

Betsy Linz thought about her twin sister, Crista. Their eighth birthday was on Friday. Betsy wanted to do something special.

"Mommy," she said. "What can I do for Crista's birthday?"

Mrs. Linz looked at Betsy. "What do you think she would like?" she asked.

Betsy thought hard. She and Crista liked all the same things—ice cream and dolls and parties.

"I'd like a party for my birthday," she said. "I think Crista would like a party too."

"You're having a party," Mrs. Linz said. "At school on Friday."

"I'd like a party at home, too," Betsy said. "And so would Crista."

"Not a big party," her mother said. "After all, we're going to go out for dinner on your birthday. You and Crista and Daddy and me and Grace and Marty."

Betsy nodded. Grace was her big sister. Marty was her little brother.

"That will be fun," she said. "But a party would be fun too."

"Your party at school will have cupcakes," Mrs. Linz said. "And all your friends will be there."

"Crista would like a party at home," Betsy said. "Not a big party. Just a little one for her birthday."

"It's your birthday too," her mother said. "Or had you forgotten?"

Betsy giggled. She and Crista shared every-thing. They slept in the same bedroom. They were in the same classes. She could never forget that they had the same birthday.

"I don't want it to be a party for me," Betsy said. "I want it to be a party for Crista."

"That's very nice of you," her mother said. "I'm

sure Crista will be pleased. Do you want to tell her now so she can help with the plans?"

Betsy and Crista did everything together. They played with Marty together. They teased Grace together. They had all the same friends.

"I want to do this by myself," Betsy said. "That way it's Crista's party and not mine."

Mrs. Linz put down the lettuce she was washing. "It sounds like you want to give Crista a surprise party."

"What's a surprise party?" Betsy asked.

"It's when you give a party for someone you love," Mrs. Linz said. "But it's a surprise. Crista won't know you're giving her a party until she comes in. Then everyone will yell 'Surprise!' "

"Will that scare Crista?" Betsy asked. Crista was scared of thunder and bugs.

"I don't think it will scare her," Mrs. Linz said. "It will startle her, and maybe she'll yell. But she won't be scared."

Betsy pictured hundreds of people yelling "Surprise!" She knew she'd be scared if too many people yelled it. And thunder and bugs didn't scare her at all, hardly.

"I don't think we should have hundreds of people," she said to her mother. She hoped her mother wouldn't be disappointed.

Her mother began washing the lettuce again. "I think you're right," she said. "Not hundreds. That would be too many."

Betsy tried to decide how many people to invite. She and Crista had lots of friends. "Do you think fifty people would be too many?" she asked.

Her mother nodded. "Way too many," she said.

"Twenty?" Betsy asked.

"Twenty would be too many, too," her mother said. "Surprise parties are very hard. If too many people are invited, then Crista is more likely to find out."

Betsy pictured twenty people yelling "Surprise!" If Crista knew about the party, it wouldn't be nearly as much fun.

"A surprise party should be small," Mrs. Linz said, "to make sure it stays a surprise."

"Is three a good number?" Betsy asked.

"Three is a perfect number," Mrs. Linz said. "That's just enough people for it to be a party. And three people can keep a secret if you tell them to."

"I'll invite Megan and Jane and Sally," Betsy said. "They're my best friends. And they're Crista's best friends too."

"Tell them to come after school on Friday," Mrs. Linz said. "When you and Crista come home, I'll take you out for ice cream. Then when we get back, you can surprise Crista."

Betsy smiled. She knew a surprise party was the nicest thing she could do for Crista.

2

Invitations

Crista and Betsy did everything together. So it wasn't easy for Betsy to tell Megan and Jane and Sally about the party.

"I think you should talk to Greg," Betsy said to Crista. They were in the school playground waiting for the bell to ring.

"Why?" Crista asked.

Betsy looked at her twin sister. Everyone said they looked exactly alike. But to Betsy, Crista looked just like Crista and nobody else.

"I don't know," Betsy said. "I just think you should."

"Do you know what I should say to him?" Crista asked.

Betsy and her mother had talked about the surprise party a lot the day before. But they hadn't talked about what Crista should say to Greg.

"You could say hi," Betsy said. "And you could tell him what happened in school yesterday. He was out sick."

"Nothing happened in school yesterday," Crista said.

"Lots of things happened," Betsy said. "We read a story. We had music."

"Greg hates music," Crista said.

"Yes, but he likes gym," Betsy said. "And we had gym yesterday."

"All right," Crista said. "I'll talk to Greg. I'll tell him about what we did in gym yesterday."

Betsy watched as her twin sister crossed the playground. Sure enough, she began talking to Greg. Betsy didn't really care what they talked about.

"Megan, Sally, come over here," she whispered.

"Sure, Betsy," they said. "What's up?"

"I'm having a surprise birthday party for Crista," Betsy said. "On Friday."

"You can't have a surprise birthday party for Crista," Megan said. "It's your birthday too."

"You can't give yourself your own party," Sally said.

"It's not my birthday party," Betsy said. "It's Crista's. And I can too. My mom says I can. So I'm inviting you and Jane."

"I see Jane over there," Sally said. "Standing by Crista and Greg."

"Go over and get her," Betsy said. "But don't let Crista know why you want her."

"What am I supposed to say?" Sally asked.

"I don't care," Betsy said. "But don't mention the party. Otherwise it won't be a surprise."

"Surprise parties seem like a big bother," Sally said. "Why do you want to give one?"

"Because I want to do something special for Crista," Betsy said. "And nobody's ever given her a surprise party before."

"I can certainly understand why," Megan said.

"I still don't know what to say to Jane," Sally said.

"Tell her Megan wants to talk to her," Betsy said. "That way Crista won't suspect anything."

So Sally went over to Jane. Whatever she said worked. Jane came over and Crista didn't seem to suspect anything.

"What do you want, Megan?" Jane asked.

"I don't want anything," Megan said. "This is all Betsy's weird idea."

"Then why did Sally say you wanted to talk to me?" Jane asked.

"To fool Crista," Betsy said.

"But Crista isn't here," Jane said. "She's over there talking with Greg."

Betsy wished her mother had warned her more about surprise parties. The party had seemed so easy when they talked about it in the kitchen.

"I sent Crista to talk to Greg," Betsy said, "so we could talk together and she wouldn't know."

"What do you want to keep from Crista?" Jane asked. "I thought the two of you told each other everything."

"We do," Betsy said.

"But you don't anymore?" Jane asked.

"Not this once," Betsy said. "This once I'm keeping something from her. I'm going to give her a surprise party."

"My father had a surprise party once," Jane said. "My mom gave it to him. We couldn't say anything to him about the party for weeks."

"Weeks before the party?" Betsy asked. She only had three days before her party and she was already going crazy.

"For weeks after the party," Jane said. "Daddy hates surprises."

"Crista loves them," Betsy said. She sure hoped Crista did. "So it's really important you don't say anything about the party to her."

"Not even a hint?" Megan asked.

Betsy thought Megan was teasing, but she wasn't sure. "Not even a hint. We're all going to surprise her on Friday."

3

Talking to Grace

After school that day, Betsy went into Grace's bedroom. Grace was twelve years old, but she liked to think she was a teenager.

"Go away," Grace said. "I never asked for a pesky little sister to bother me."

"I need to talk to you," Betsy said. "It isn't for me. It's for Crista."

"Crista's a pesky little sister too," Grace said. "But she's less pesky than you are. What do you think about this nail-polish color?"

"It's very red," Betsy said. She climbed on Grace's bed so she could see better.

"Do you think Mom will let me wear it?" Grace asked. "Or do you think she'll say it's too red?"

"I think she'll say it's too red," Betsy said.

"Couldn't you put some white in it so it would be pink?"

"I don't have any white nail polish," Grace said.

"We have white shoe polish," Betsy said. "You could mix the nail polish and the shoe polish. That way your nails and your shoes would be the same color."

"Sometimes you are unusually silly," Grace said. But then she giggled. "Dad would love that. He'd polish his white shoes and they'd end up pink."

"I guess it wasn't a good idea," Betsy said. "But Mom still won't let you wear such red nail polish."

"Maybe she will when I'm thirteen," Grace said. "I have a birthday in three months."

"I have one on Friday," Betsy said.

"Oh, do you?" Grace said. "I must have forgotten."

"Crista and I both do," Betsy said. "That's what I wanted to talk to you about."

"I thought you wanted to talk about nail polish," Grace said.

"No," Betsy said. "That was what you wanted to talk about."

"I didn't want to talk to you about anything," Grace said. "You came in here, remember?"

Betsy was very glad she was twelve minutes older than Crista. Grace was enough big sister for anybody.

"I'm giving Crista a surprise birthday party on Friday," Betsy said. "I've invited Megan and Jane and Sally and they're all coming."

"You really expect Jane to keep it a secret?" Grace asked. "Jane never keeps anything a secret."

"She'll keep this a secret," Betsy said. "I told her she had to."

"She told everybody last year her mother was going to have a baby," Grace said, "months before her mother wanted people to know."

"But that's different," Betsy said. She sure hoped it was different. She'd forgotten what a terrible time Jane had keeping secrets.

"I think you should make sure Jane doesn't

spend much time with Crista," Grace said. "It's only until Friday."

"That's a good idea," Betsy said. "If I see Jane and Crista talking together, I could tell Crista to go away."

"Crista'll love that," Grace said. "Maybe you should try a different approach."

Betsy wrinkled her nose. She did that when she had to think hard about something. Crista frowned when she had to think about something. That was one way people told them apart.

"I could stay with Crista all the time between now and Friday," Betsy said. "That way she won't have a chance to talk to Jane."

"Crista would find that very boring," Grace said. "I would find that very boring, spending all my time with you."

"I could spend all my time with Jane," Betsy said. "But Crista would wonder why. Jane's one of my best friends, but I don't like her that much."

"Why not just keep an eye on Jane?" Grace said. "Then if you see her talking with Crista, you could go over. You could make sure Jane doesn't mention the party."

"That's a good idea," Betsy said. "And I could tell Megan and Sally to keep an eye on Jane too."

"Good idea," Grace said. "Crista will be less likely to suspect then."

Betsy smiled. This surprise-party business was looking better and better.

"I still don't know why you came in here," Grace said. "Unless it was to bother me."

"I came to invite you," Betsy said, "to Crista's surprise party."

"Oh," Grace said. "Thank you. That's very nice."

"So you'll come?" Betsy asked.

"I'd be happy to," Grace said.

"And you won't tell Crista?" Betsy asked.

"I promise I won't," Grace said.

Betsy smiled. Crista was going to have the best surprise party ever given.

4

Whispers

Betsy and Crista and Grace took turns helping their parents make supper. That day it was Crista's turn to help their mother cook, and Betsy's turn to set the table, and Grace's turn to help wash dishes with their father.

Betsy put the plates on the table. She could smell the chicken her mother was cooking. Chicken was her favorite.

Helping their mother cook was Crista's favorite thing. Usually Betsy could hear the two of them talking while she set the table. But that evening she could hardly hear what they were saying.

Betsy realized they were whispering. What could Crista be whispering about? It had to be something she didn't want Betsy to know.

Was Mom telling Crista about the surprise party? Maybe she was worried the party would scare Crista. If they all yelled "Surprise!" at the same time, maybe Crista would get scared by the loud noise.

Betsy stopped folding napkins so she could listen more carefully. She'd never noticed how noisy napkin folding could be.

"Whisper whisper," Crista whispered.

"Whisper whisper," Mrs. Linz whispered back.

Betsy wasn't sure, but she thought she heard her mother say, "Surprise party." And she wasn't positive, but she thought she heard Crista say, "Friday."

"What are you doing?"

Betsy turned around and saw her father standing in the dining room. He was holding Marty. Marty wanted to get down, so he began to cry.

"Shush, Marty," Mr. Linz said. He gave Marty a kiss on his forehead. Marty only squiggled some more.

"Marty wants to get down," Betsy said.

"I know," Mr. Linz said. "But I thought I'd put him in his high chair. It's almost time for supper."

"Whaaa!" Marty screamed. Marty was a very good screamer. Betsy was glad he was too young to understand about surprise parties. He'd be sure to scream about it if he knew.

Mr. Linz put Marty in the high chair. Marty screamed some more, then he stopped. Supper smelled good to him, too.

"What were you doing, Betsy?" her father asked.

"I was folding napkins," Betsy said.

"That's funny," her father said. "It looked to me like you were eavesdropping."

"I was not," Betsy said. "What's eavesdropping?"

"When you listen to somebody else's conversation," her father said. "The way you were listening to Mom and Crista's."

"Oh," Betsy said. "Then maybe I was eavesdropping. But I had to."

"Why?" her father asked.

"Because I couldn't hear what they were saying otherwise," Betsy said.

Her father laughed. "Maybe they didn't want you to hear," he said.

"I don't think that's right," Betsy said. "Crista and I never have secrets."

"Maybe it wasn't Crista's secret," her father said. "Maybe it was your mother's."

"Do you think so?" Betsy asked.

"Maybe," Mr. Linz said. "But whatever it was, they didn't want you to hear. And you should never eavesdrop. It's rude to."

"I won't do it again," Betsy said.

"Good," her father said. "Boy, dinner smells great." He went into the kitchen. Crista came out.

"What were you talking about with Daddy?" Crista asked. She picked up the forks and started putting them on the napkins. It wasn't her day to set the table, but she helped anyway.

"Nothing," Betsy said. "He taught me a new word. Eavesdropping. It means listening."

"Oh," Crista said.

"What were you talking to Mom about?" Betsy asked.

"Nothing," Crista said. She took the knives next and put them by the plates.

"I thought I could hear you whispering," Betsy said.

"Maybe we were whispering," Crista said. "I don't remember."

Betsy didn't see how anybody could forget whispering. She gave Crista a funny look.

But Crista didn't seem to notice. Instead she finished setting the table. And then she smiled.

Betsy wished she knew why Crista was smiling. But it was hard to eavesdrop on a smile.

5

The Big Joke

Betsy and Crista walked to school the next day. Sometimes Betsy thought about the surprise party. When she did, she smiled. Sometimes Crista smiled. Crista's smile made Betsy very nervous.

"Why are you smiling?" Betsy asked.

"I don't know," Crista said. "You've been smiling too. Why are you smiling?"

"I don't know," Betsy said.

"Well, I'm smiling for the same reason," Crista said. "Oh, there's Sally and Megan. I need to talk to them."

"About what?" Betsy asked.

"Nothing," Crista said. "Why don't you talk to Greg?"

"What should I say to Greg?" Betsy asked.

"You could talk to him about baseball," Crista said. "You both love baseball. I bet Greg has lots of interesting things to say about baseball."

Betsy liked Greg. She liked baseball. She liked talking with Greg about baseball. But she didn't like the way Crista was acting.

"I see Jane," Betsy said. "Maybe I'll talk to Jane instead."

"No," Crista said. "I need to talk to Jane too."

"What do you need to talk to Jane about?" Betsy asked.

"Nothing," Crista said. "I just do. Why don't you talk to Greg while I talk to Sally and Megan?"

"All right," Betsy said. She wished she knew why Crista was acting so funny.

"Hi, Betsy," Greg said. "Did you watch the baseball game last night?"

"Only a little bit," Betsy said. "Then I had to go to bed."

"I listened to the game in my bedroom," Greg

said. "When I keep the radio really low, my mom doesn't always hear."

"I can't do that," Betsy said. "Crista would hear. She doesn't like baseball as much as I do."

"It was a good game," Greg said. "Or at least it was until the fourth inning. That's when I fell asleep."

"That's nice," Betsy said. She could see Crista talking with Megan and Sally. She couldn't tell what they were talking about. But she could tell Megan and Sally were giggling.

"I see Jane," Betsy said to Greg. "I have to talk to her. I'll see you later."

"Okay," Greg said. Betsy ran over to Jane.

"You told Crista about the surprise party, didn't you?" Betsy said.

"I did not," Jane said. "I would never give away a secret."

"You give away secrets all the time," Betsy said. She looked over at Crista and the others. They were still talking and giggling.

"Well, I don't mean to," Jane said. "Anyway, I

didn't give this one away. I haven't told Crista anything."

"Good," Betsy said. "See to it you don't."

"Honestly, Betsy," Jane said. "You were a lot nicer before you started giving this party."

"You were a lot nicer before I invited you," Betsy said.

"I don't want you to be my friend anymore," Jane said.

"I don't want you to be my friend either," Betsy said. "But you still have to come to the party."

"Why?" Jane asked.

"Because you're still Crista's friend," Betsy said.

"In that case I might as well still be your friend," Jane said.

Betsy nodded. "Thank you," she said. "I want us to still be friends. I just worry about Crista finding out about the party."

"She won't hear it from me," Jane said.

Just then Megan walked over to them. "Hi, Jane," she said. "Sally wants to talk to you about something."

"About what?" Jane asked.

"I don't know," Megan said. "She just told me to come here and get you."

"Doesn't she want to talk to me, too?" Betsy asked.

"No," Megan said. "Just Jane."

"I don't think that's right," Jane said. "Betsy and I are friends."

"Will you just come with me?" Megan said. "Betsy understands. Don't you, Betsy?"

"I understand," Betsy said. She watched as Megan and Jane walked over to Sally and Crista. When Jane got there, Sally told her something. Jane giggled.

Betsy was sure she understood then. Someone had told Crista about the surprise party. And now everyone thought it was a big joke on her.

6

Giggles

Betsy spent Thursday looking for proof that Crista knew about the party.

She watched very carefully every time Crista talked with Megan or Sally or Jane. Especially Jane.

Crista seemed to giggle a lot when she talked with their friends. Their friends seemed to giggle even more.

Every time one of them giggled, Betsy got more and more nervous. What could they be giggling about if it wasn't the surprise party?

So after school Betsy went first to Megan. "Did you tell Crista about the surprise party?" she asked.

"I did not," Megan said. But she giggled.

Then Betsy went to Sally. "Did you tell Crista about the surprise party?" she asked.

"Of course not," Sally said. But she giggled.

Finally Betsy went to Jane. "Did you tell Crista about the surprise party?" she asked.

"I told you I wouldn't," Jane said. But she giggled.

"Did anybody else tell her?" Betsy asked. If Jane knew, she'd probably tell.

Jane shook her head. "We're all very good at keeping secrets," she said. "No matter how many we've been told."

As far as Betsy knew, they'd only been told one secret. But maybe they'd been told other secrets so secret no one had told Betsy.

When Betsy and Crista walked home from school, Betsy tried to find out what Crista knew. "Tomorrow's our birthday," Betsy began.

"I know that," Crista said. She looked nervous.

"Do you think we'll have fun?" Betsy asked.

"Of course we will," Crista said. "We'll have a party at school. With cupcakes. And then we'll all go out for supper together."

"Do you think that's all that's going to happen?" Betsy asked.

"No," Crista said.

"Aha!" Betsy said. "What else do you think is going to happen?"

"I think Mom and Dad and Grace will give us presents," Crista said. "And Dad will bake us a birthday cake."

"Chocolate," Betsy said. "Daddy only bakes chocolate cake."

"That's okay," Crista said. "Chocolate's my favorite."

"Mine too," Betsy said.

The girls were silent for a moment.

"I think that sounds like a very nice birthday," Crista finally said. "A party at school and presents and supper out and cake."

"Me too," Betsy said. "We don't need anything more than that."

"I don't," Crista said. "I'll be very happy with a birthday like that."

"I'll be very happy too," Betsy said. Actually,

she thought a birthday like that sounded pretty boring. What it really needed was a surprise party. It was a good thing she was giving one.

When they got home, Marty was in his playpen. He stood up when the twins came in. Then he threw his favorite teddy bear at them.

"That means he loves you," Mrs. Linz said. Crista picked up the teddy bear and gave it back to Marty.

"I love him too," Crista said. She gave Marty a kiss. "Mommy, could I talk to you for a minute? Alone?"

"Of course," Mrs. Linz said.

Betsy watched as they walked into the kitchen together. What did Crista have to say to their mother? Did she hate the idea of a surprise party? Was she trying to get it called off?

She could hear Crista and their mother whisper. But this time she didn't try to listen. She just stood still until they came back to the living room.

"Mommy, can I talk to you alone too?" Betsy asked.

"Of course," Mrs. Linz said.

So Betsy and her mother went into the kitchen.

"I'm worried about my surprise party," Betsy whispered.

"What are you worried about?" her mother asked.

"I'm worried that Crista knows about it," Betsy said. "She's been acting funny lately."

"No funnier than you," her mother said.

"But I have a very good reason to act funny," Betsy said. "I'm giving her a surprise party."

"Maybe Crista has a very good reason too," Mrs. Linz said.

"What?" Betsy asked.

But her mother only giggled.

7

Birthday Kittens

"Happy birthday!" Mrs. Linz said to Betsy first thing the next morning. She gave Betsy a kiss.

"Happy birthday!" Mrs. Linz said next to Crista. She gave Crista a kiss too.

"Happy birthday, Crista!" Betsy said.

"Happy birthday, Betsy!" Crista said.

Betsy loved birthdays. She decided she didn't care if Crista knew about the surprise party. It was still going to be the best birthday ever.

The girls got dressed really fast. At breakfast, Grace gave each of them a gift.

"Happy birthday," she said. "These gifts are from Marty and me."

Betsy hoped Marty had picked them out. Grace

had terrible taste. She opened her present. It was a doll dressed in a funny costume.

"It's from Spain," Grace said. "That's what people wear in Spain."

The doll's dress was as red as Grace's nail polish. "Thank you, Grace," Betsy said. "I'll name her something Spanish."

Crista opened her present next. It was another doll dressed in another funny costume.

"It's from Holland," Grace said. "That's what they wear in Holland. See the wooden shoes."

"Thank you, Grace," Crista said. "I think I'll name her Holly since she's from Holland."

Betsy wished she'd been that smart. But Spainy was a funny name anyway. It sounded like something you cleaned floors with.

"I'll see you at school this afternoon," their mother said. "I'll be sure to bring cupcakes."

Betsy and Crista smiled. Birthdays were the best kind of day in the world.

At school they mostly did school things. They each read and they added and subtracted. In gym, they played kickball. All their friends wished them a happy birthday. Megan and Sally and Jane all giggled.

After lunch, the twins had their party. Mrs. Linz brought in the cupcakes. Everyone sang "Happy Birthday." Betsy and Crista handed one cupcake to each kid in the class. They gave one to their teacher as well.

Betsy wondered what it was like not to have a twin to share your birthday with. She bet it wasn't nearly as much fun.

She and Crista ran home after school. Mrs. Linz was waiting for them outside with Marty. "Let's get some ice cream," Mrs. Linz said. "To celebrate."

So they all went out for ice cream. Mrs. Linz let the twins each get a cone with two scoops just because it was their birthday.

They walked home slowly together. Marty was in his stroller, but he liked to look around. Betsy was scared about what would happen when they got home.

Suppose nobody came to Crista's surprise party? Suppose it wasn't a surprise anymore?

"I have a surprise for your birthday," Mrs. Linz said as they walked by Mrs. Schultz's house.

Betsy got even more nervous. Was her mother going to tell Crista about the party?

"Mrs. Schultz's cat had kittens," Mrs. Linz said instead. "You can each have one as your special birthday present."

"My own kitten?" Betsy asked.

"A kitten just for me?" Crista asked.

Mrs. Linz laughed. "A kitten for each one of you," she said. She knocked on Mrs. Schultz's door. Mrs. Schultz opened it right away. "We're here to meet Pokey's kittens," Mrs. Linz said.

"Come on in, girls," Mrs. Schultz said. "And happy birthday. The kittens are in the kitchen with their mama."

Betsy, Crista, and their mother followed Mrs. Schultz. Sure enough, in the kitchen were six little kittens and one big mama cat.

"The kittens are a little too young to leave their

mother," Mrs. Schultz said. "But in two weeks, they'll be the right age. Why don't you each pick one now? You can come over and play with them until they're ready to go home with you."

Betsy picked a black kitten with a white face. Crista picked a gray kitten with a white face.

"Say good-bye to your kittens, girls," Mrs. Linz said. "We have to go home now."

So the girls did. They ran back to the house. Betsy was so excited, she forgot what was waiting for them.

"SURPRISE!"

Betsy didn't know who jumped higher, her or Crista.

S

Surprise Party!

"Surprise, Crista!" Betsy said. "I gave you a surprise party."

"Happy birthday, Crista!" Megan and Jane and Sally and Grace all said.

"A surprise party?" Crista said. She sank onto the living-room sofa.

"Do you like it?" Betsy asked. "I hope it didn't scare you."

"It didn't scare me," Crista said. "It's wonderful. Thank you, Betsy."

"Mom helped," Betsy said. "And everybody kept it a secret. I was so worried you knew about it."

"I didn't know a thing," Crista said. "Our friends are great secret keepers."

"That's what I kept saying," Jane said. "But Betsy never believed me."

"Now I do," Betsy said.

"Come on, girls," Mrs. Linz said. "I have lots of games for you to play."

So the girls played Pin the Tail on the Donkey. Then they played Musical Chairs. Grace didn't play the games. They were too babyish for her. But she helped Mrs. Linz set things up. And she rooted for the twins to win.

The girls played with Marty. He'd walk to one of them and then he'd stumble. One of the girls would pick him up and get him walking again. Sometimes they'd kiss him. Marty didn't seem to mind.

"Marty has three girlfriends," Mrs. Linz said.

"Baby brothers are cute," Sally said. "I wish I had a baby brother."

"I wish I had a twin," Jane said.

"I wish I had a puppy," Megan said.

"We're getting kittens!" Betsy said. "Mommy, can we go over and see our kittens?"

"If you're all very careful," Mrs. Linz said. "Grace, would you take the girls? I need to set things up here."

"Sure," Grace said. She was never that nice normally. Betsy wished she had birthdays more often.

The six girls went to Mrs. Schultz's house. Pokey the cat was washing her kittens when they got there.

"The gray one is mine," Crista said. "I'm going to name her Misty because she's gray."

"The black-and-white one is mine," Betsy said. She wished she'd thought of a great name already.

"It needs a name," Megan said. "If I had a puppy, I'd name it Prince."

"What if it was a girl?" Sally asked.

"Then I'd name it Princess," Megan said.

"I think Misty's a prettier name," Jane said. "You should give your kitten a pretty name, Betsy."

"I will," Betsy said. "When I think of one."

"Come on, girls," Grace said. "We'd better go back home. Mom has cookies and milk waiting."

The girls all started back to the Linz house. Betsy cast one last look at her kitten. It was so cute, it really deserved a name.

"It's too close to supper for cake," Mrs. Linz said. "But you can each have some cookies. Happy birthday, Betsy and Crista."

"Happy birthday!" everybody shouted. Even Marty said, "Huppup buppup."

Betsy ate a chocolate-chip cookie. "Chocolate-chip cookies are my favorite," she said. "I'm going to name my kitten Chips."

"What a good name!" Crista said. "Misty and Chips. Those are perfect names for our kittens."

"They are, aren't they?" Betsy said. She felt very pleased with herself. She hoped Chips would be able to tell her apart from Crista. Twins might be hard on kittens.

After cookies and milk, the girls went outside to play. They played hide-and-seek. Then they played tag.

"Time to go home!" Mrs. Linz called to them. "Your mothers are all here."

So the girls went back inside. Soon everybody had left.

Betsy looked at Crista. "How did you like your surprise party?" Betsy asked.

"I thought it was wonderful," Crista said.

But then she did something funny.

She giggled.

9
Twin Surprises

When Mr. Linz came home from work, they all went out to supper.

Mom dressed Marty in his best overalls. Betsy and Crista each got to wear her favorite dress. And even Grace got to wear red nail polish.

"What a nice-looking family I have," Mr. Linz said.

"And what a nice family, too," Mrs. Linz said.

"I meant that," Mr. Linz said. He kissed Mrs. Linz.

It took a while to get them all into the station wagon. Then when they got to the restaurant, it took a while for them all to get out. Marty was cute, but his car seat took forever.

The twins had gotten to pick where they wanted to eat. They had agreed they wanted to eat at Tony's. It was their favorite restaurant.

"Try not to get sauce on your dresses," Mrs. Linz said. "Or on your tie," she said to her husband.

It was hard to eat carefully, but Betsy did. She got spaghetti with meat sauce. Crista got spaghetti with meatballs. Neither one of them got dirty.

Marty got a hamburger with French fries. After a while, he threw his French fries at people. Grace caught most of them.

"I never asked for a little brother," she said.

It was the first time all day she sounded like Grace. Betsy guessed that meant the birthday was coming to an end.

"I woke up this morning before everybody else," Mr. Linz said, "so I could bake you a birthday cake. Guess what kind it is?"

"Chocolate!" they all shouted.

Mr. Linz looked surprised. "It is," he said. "How did you know?"

"Because chocolate's our favorite," Crista said. "So we knew you'd make it for us."

"Besides, that's the only kind you ever make," Betsy said.

Mr. Linz smiled. "It's a good thing it's your favorite then," he said. "I made peanut-butter icing to go with it."

"Peanut-butter icing!" Betsy said. "That's my favorite thing in the world."

"I thought chocolate-chip cookies were," Grace said. "Maybe you should name your kitten Peanut Butter."

"I can't wait to meet these kittens," Mr. Linz said. "It sounds like it's been quite a birthday."

"It isn't over yet," Mrs. Linz said. "Come on, everybody. Let's go back home and eat Daddy's cake."

So they packed themselves up and got back into the station wagon. Marty still had French fries in his hands. He threw them at his sisters during the ride home.

The house was all brightly lit when they got back. "I left some lights on," Mrs. Linz said, "so it wouldn't be too dark when we got in."

"Good idea," Mr. Linz said. He lifted Marty out of his car seat and carried him into the kitchen.

"Crista, Betsy, go into your bedroom and change into your pajamas," Mrs. Linz said.

"But it's too early to go to bed," Betsy said. "We haven't had our cake yet."

"I didn't say you had to go to bed," her mother said. "Just that you should change into your pajamas."

"Come on, Betsy," Crista said. "We don't want to get cake on our dresses."

Betsy looked around at her family. Grace was giggling. Mr. and Mrs. Linz were giggling. Crista was giggling. The only person who wasn't giggling was Marty.

"All right," Betsy said. She followed Crista down the hallway to their dark bedroom. Crista turned on the light.

"SURPRISE!"

There, in their pajamas, were Megan and Sally and Jane.

"What?" Betsy asked. She'd never been so surprised in her life.

"I'm giving you a surprise sleepover party," Crista said. "Are you sure you didn't guess?"

"I didn't guess a thing," Betsy said. She wondered if her heart would ever stop pounding.

"Mommy said I could on Tuesday," Crista said. "And I invited everybody on Wednesday before school."

"See," Jane said. "And you thought I couldn't keep a secret. I kept two!"

"You should have seen your face, Betsy," Sally said. "You looked as startled as Crista did this afternoon."

"Come on, girls!" Mrs. Linz called. "It's time for birthday cake!"

The Linz twins left their bedroom with their three best friends walking beside them. Two dolls, two kittens, two surprise parties. Betsy smiled. Being a twin was the best thing in the world.

She looked at Crista and Crista looked at her. And then they both giggled.